TAKE FLIGHT AND FIGHT!

by Hannah S. Campbell

illustrated by Caravan Studio

Grosset & Dunlap
An Imprint of Penguin Group (USA) LLC

GROSSET & DUNLAP
Published by the Penguin Group
Penguin Group (USA) LLC, 375 Hudson Street, New York, New York 10014, USA

USA | Canada | UK | Ireland | Australia | New Zealand | India | South Africa | China

penguin.com
A Penguin Random House Company

ISBN 978-0-448-48486-0   10 9 8 7 6 5 4 3 2 1

It was a beautiful sunny day in Skylands, and several dragon Skylanders were gathered at Dragon's Peak for an afternoon of fun.

"It's nice to be able to get some rest and relaxation without Kaos's Trolls on our case!" said Flashwing. "And my crystals sure look nice in this sunlight, don't they?"

Flashwing was a dragon of the Earth Element with sparkling gemstone wings. Each dragon had an Element that gave him or her unique powers.

"Well, I, for one, would prefer a bit of action!" said Cynder, scowling at Flashwing. "I hate wasting my electric energy relaxing while Kaos is still out there!" Cynder was pacing underneath a large umbrella to avoid the sunshine. Like most Skylanders of the Undead Element, Cynder preferred spending time in the dark.

"I know!" said Spyro, a purple Magic dragon. "Let's have a race! I've heard stories about a treasure at the very top of Dragon's Peak. How about whoever reaches it first gets to keep it?" Spyro was a natural leader, so the other dragons were quick to agree to his plan.

"A valiant quest for treasure, you say?" said Blades. "I accept this challenge!"

Blades was a knightly Air dragon with sharp, shiny armor and a sword on his tail.

Fire Kraken, a dragon of the Fire Element, puffed out his chest in response.

"I'll blaze a trail all the way to the top!" he said, bouncing around on his tail.

"We'll see if any of you can take the heat!"

The dragons spent hours running, jumping, and flying around the island, searching for the shortest path to the top. Dragons are some of the fastest creatures in Skylands, so the race was very close. In the end, the winner was Zap, an electric-blue Water dragon.

"Power surge!" he said with a gurgle as he slid up to the treasure on a trail of electric Sea Slime. "Victory is mine!"

Later, the tired dragons sat down to rest and talk about their favorite battles.

"But just when I thought I was a goner, I threw a fireball back at the gang of Trolls and flew right up to the castle!" Spyro said excitedly, remembering his latest trip to the evil Kaos's fortress.

"Not too shabby," said Camo, a bright green Life dragon. "Almost as good as that time I took out a bunch of Kaos's Spell Punks with just a few Sun Blasts! It must be all that strength and speed I've cultivated from training—and a steady diet of fruits and vegetables."

"Too bad you can't fly—you could have taken on Kaos himself!" joked Cynder. "Better leave that battle for the *real* dragons."

Camo's face fell. Cynder was only kidding, but flight was a sensitive subject among dragons.

"That's not fair!" said Zap. "We wingless dragons are just as important as anybody else. After all, which one of us just won the treasure race? And there's nobody better than a Water dragon when you need to cross a giant waterfall or lagoon."

"Your victory was a mere fluke!" said Blades. "We Air dragons are built for soaring and gliding on the wind—high above any waterfall or lagoon! I daresay I would win in a rematch."

"Who needs Water or flying when you have FIRE?" roared Fire Kraken. "*Fire and dragons* go together like peanut butter and jelly!" he said, shooting off sparks as he spoke.

"My technical enhancements are superior to fire, peanut butter, or jelly," argued Drobot, a Tech dragon with robotic armor.

It seemed like the dragons' argument would never come to an end.

Suddenly, the face of Master Eon, a great Portal Master, appeared above the group of arguing dragons. They fell silent when they saw him, for all Skylanders have the greatest respect for Master Eon and his wisdom.

"Skylanders," he said solemnly, "you are needed on Frogbillows Island. A group of cyclopses has arrived, and they are determined to destroy the Mabu villages so that Kaos will be able to build a new outpost. Due to a mysterious enchantment, only dragons can land safely on the island. Please, come quickly to the Portal!"

The dragons knew that this was serious. Kaos was a terrible villain who would stop at nothing in his quest to rule Skylands.

"Walloping watermelons! We can't let this happen!" growled Camo.

"Kaos should know better than to mess with the dragons!"
Spyro said, breathing an angry puff of smoke from his nostrils.

"Master Eon, we are prepared to deploy!" Drobot responded.

"Let us advance to the Portal."

Master Eon transported the Skylanders to Frogbillows Island, where the destruction had already begun.

"These cyclopses are indeed a crew of formidable foes," Blades said with a scowl as he used his Wing Slice to stop a pair of spinning Mohawk Cyclopses.

Fire Kraken then showered a colorful fireworks attack over their heads, and quickly bounced up, avoiding the cyclopses' axes. "Ha! They won't mess with my fire now—or your sharp wings," he said to Blades. "Let's do it again!"

Meanwhile, Cynder and Camo teamed up to fight a group of Cyclops Sleetthrowers. Every time the cyclopses threw a shovelful of snow at the Skylanders, Cynder melted it with a bright blast of Spectral Lightning. Then, Camo used the melted snow to grow thick vines filled with explosive peppers and watermelons. The fruits and veggies burst in their enemies' faces as Cynder and Camo kept filling the air with electric volts and flashes of light.

All around Frogbillows Island, the dragons fought side by side to battle the cyclopses and save the Mabu. Zap spread the ground with electrified Sea Slime, while Drobot flung his spinning Tactical Bladegears at the monsters stuck in the slime.

Flashwing filled the air with Crystal Shards, which reflected the light from Spyro's flying fireballs. The cyclopses tried to shield their huge single eyes from the bright flames, but they could not escape.

All the Elements came together, bringing the cyclopses' attack to a sudden stop.

"What has happened?" shouted a shrill voice from the center of the island. "Why have my cyclops minions stopped their work?" It was Kaos! But when he saw the Skylanders standing where the cyclopses had been, he stopped short.

"Surprised to see us, Kaos?" Spyro laughed.

Kaos looked around, hoping to find more of his servants in the area.

"S-s-surprised?" he stuttered, clearly caught off guard. "Why should I be worried? I have more minions in Skylands than you all have scales on your bodies!" he boasted, turning up his nose at them.

"That may be true," said Cynder. "But I don't see any of them here. Do you really think you can take all of us on your own?" Cynder sent out a shock of lightning as a warning, and Drobot's robotic gears clanked, preparing for action.

The rest of the dragons lowered their bodies, ready to pounce.

Kaos backed up slowly, but as the fierce dragons came closer, he quickly turned and ran to his Portal.

"Shall we give chase?" asked Blades.

"Eh, let's give him a head start," said Flashwing. "He sure needs it!"

As Kaos ran to the Portal, the dragons suddenly remembered the argument they'd been having earlier that day.

"I'm sorry I made jokes about you not being able to fly, Camo," said Cynder. "I couldn't have taken those guys without your potent peppers."

"No problem," Camo said. "Who knew that Life and Undead together would lead to such a scrumptious victory?"

"Or Water and Tech?" said Drobot to Zap. "I predicted that your slime would destroy my robotic gears. However, my reports indicate the result was actually quite electrifying!"

"Well, I think we've given that pesky Kaos enough time to even the playing field," said Flashwing. "I could take him by myself, of course, but I think we work better as a team. Shall we?" Flashwing was never one to be modest, but inside, she was glad to be fighting together with the other dragons.

"I'm all fired up and ready to go!" said Spyro, rising into the air.

The other dragons followed suit, running, bouncing, and flying to Kaos's Portal, ready to bring justice to Skylands once again.